T0199037

Kindness is MY Superpower!

Elyse M. Dawson

Illustrated by: Bethany Buckner

Leah's recital

Daddy's home!

our family

Dedicated to: Eden & Jackson

You are an answer to prayer. Remember that anything is possible with God. Thank you for teaching me about kindness every day.

Love Mom!

Kindness is MY Superpower!

"He has told you, O man, what is good;

And what does the Lord require of you

Except to be just, and to love [and to diligently

practice] kindness (compassion),

And to walk humbly with your God-"

Micah 6:8 (AMP)

Did you know that kindness is a superpower? It lives in you and me. It waits to be discovered, and it gives out generously. It doesn't matter how old you are. It doesn't matter where you are from.

It doesn't matter how different you are. What matters is that kindness is for everyone! Let me show you some ways, that this superpower of kindness can be displayed.

One act of kindness can save...

A giving heart does not go unnoticed. Especially to this little girl, and her dog named Otis. A cup of cold water can save a life. It might seem small, but this superpower is bigger than us all!

One act of kindness can bring SO MUCH JOY...

Maddie loves when you pet her and scratch behind her ears. It fills her heart with great joy to know that you are near. The light in her eyes and the pep in her step, is just one reason we show kindness to our pets!

Dogs know how to "warm" their way into our hearts, and affections. It's for the best, although she is very protective! Maddie we love you, you've enriched our lives. We brought home a new brother for you. Here is Ranger boy, also-a superhero in disguise!

One act of
kindness can
make someone
brave...

The teacher said, "In 10 more minutes Ryan, you will give your speech on frogs!" I saw my friend Ryan green in the face, sit down and nod. All of a sudden, my superpower revved up at maximum speed! Asking, " How are you?" Can make a BIG difference, and fill a BIG need!

"Ryan, I know this is very hard, but I won't be far. You will do really great!" Then Ryan started to feel quite brave. The green look in his face disappeared, as confidence filled the air–because of the one act of kindness that was shared.

One act of kindness can heal...

Your words bring healing, hope, and joy. You may not understand just yet, the power of holding your Nana's hand. The sweet kisses you give her on her cheek, even now when she is feeling weak.

Your voice may be small, but it sure is mighty! Your words of kindness, and love are ever binding. As you bind her hurting heart, you are also fueling her body with a powerful art!

One act of kindness can bring comfort...

Beautiful flowers with red and blue hues. They may be wild, but then again so are you. They are unique, and wonderful in every way. Just like you, this made my day! I can clearly see your superpower, behind this beautiful bouquet of wildflowers.

The superpower did its job, because now I feel comforted and very loved. When you think of someone let them know it. Find some way to really show it. It can be as simple, or as thoughtful as a smile. Just knowing someone cares can bring lasting hope and comfort, for a long, long, while.

One act of kindness can make this world a better place...

"What if they are mean to me Mom?" That is a good question dear one. I know it can hurt when others choose to be mean. Remember who you are, and what you believe. Kindness has an amazing story to tell. Sometimes kids are mean, because they are hurting as well.

I believe that kindness plants a seed we cannot see. We water it in faith, love, and maturity. Always treat others the way you'd want to be treated. If you see a need, I challenge you dear one to meet it. People matter; even those who are hurting. We all need a little bit of hope, called kindness. Each one is deserving!

One act of kindness can give us strength...

Mikey's mom is in the Army, and so is my dad. They are both deployed during the holidays, and we are feeling sad. Something I do to help me get through, is to think of a way to help a friend find their strength. It fills a hole in my heart with purpose and meaning, to do something that is very fulfilling!

From sword fights, tag, and delicious cookies-to inviting Mikey over, to watch some really cool movies. It's nice to know that I don't have to face life alone. An act of kindness made us friends. Kindness is in NO WAY a weakness!

One act of kindness can bring peace...

It's easy to feel afraid and worried. To have a big mission and be in a hurry. Peace will help quiet your mind and calm your fears. Peace will remind you to slow down because God is near.

Here is some soup and yummy bread, even superhero's need their rest. Knowing when to rest and when to go, is the key for real superhero growth. Right now it's important that you eat. Pretty soon you'll be up off this couch and back on your feet!

Kindness is like a compass and a really good teacher. Kindness will point the way with every new venture. Life will have its ups and downs, but kindness will help hold you steady, with both feet on the ground.

Never forget who you. You are brilliant, brave, beautiful, and strong. In everything, give thanks with a grateful heart. God is good, faithful and true. He will always take good care of me and you!

Doggie hugs♡

te park

what a mess

camping with Mikey

incess Starie
vs
ace monsters

WestBow Press books may be ordered through booksellers or by contacting:

WestBow Press
A Division of Thomas Nelson & Zondervan
1663 Liberty Drive
Bloomington, IN 47403
www.westbowpress.com
1 (866) 928-1240

Scripture quotations are taken from the Amplified® Bible, Copyright © 2015 by The Lockman Foundation. Used by permission.

ISBN: 978-1-9736-9390-1 (sc)
ISBN: 978-1-9736-9391-8 (e)

Library of Congress Control Number: 2020910776

Print information available on the last page.

WestBow Press rev. date: 6/30/2020

WestBow
PRESS®
A DIVISION OF THOMAS NELSON
& ZONDERVAN

Printed in the United States
By Bookmasters